Curtis Jobling & Tom McLaughlin

# The Sheep won't Sleep!

EGMONT

The stars above the farm shine bright
As Sheepdog turns in for the night.
A hundred sheep now put to bed,
He yawns and shakes his weary head.

But . . .

# THE SHEEP WON'T SLEEP!

They're causing chaos once again.
Can you count them? I see ten!

Within the barn, upon the floor,
Hen is roosting in the straw.

Not so far from dear old Hen,
Pig is snoring in his pen.

But . . .

# THE SHEEP WON'T SLEEP!

Startled squawks and eggs aplenty,
Feathers flying, there go **twenty!**
Getting grubby, down and dirty,
Another ten we're up to **thirty!**

Over ground and under furrow
The rabbits rest inside their burrow.

But . . .

# THE SHEEP WON'T SLEEP!

Flopping, hopping,
  oh so naughty,
They just keep coming,
  count 'em, **forty!**

Dodging all the giddy deeds,
Goose is hiding in the reeds.

The moon is high, the hour is late,
Goat is napping by the gate.

But . . .

THE SHEEP WON'T SLEEP!

Splishing, splashing, naughty, nifty,
Shifty sheep now number **fifty!**
Ten more bleating, being tricksy,
Woolly jumpers just hit **sixty!**

Have we found a peaceful bed?
Cow is snoozing in her shed.

But . . .

# THE SHEEP WON'T SLEEP!

Udders swinging, moos aplenty,
Funky flock approaching **seventy!**

Keep those peepers firmly peeled,
Bull is dozing in his field!

And as we close our fluffy fable,
Horse is napping in his stable.

But . . .

# THE SHEEP WON'T SLEEP!

Charge for safety, very hasty,
Hurdling hedges go our **eighty!**

Hooves that hammer,
loud and mighty,
Another ten and
here come **ninety!**

The farmhouse seems the place to hide,
As Sheepdog takes a peek outside.

But . . .

# THE SHEEP WON'T SLEEP!

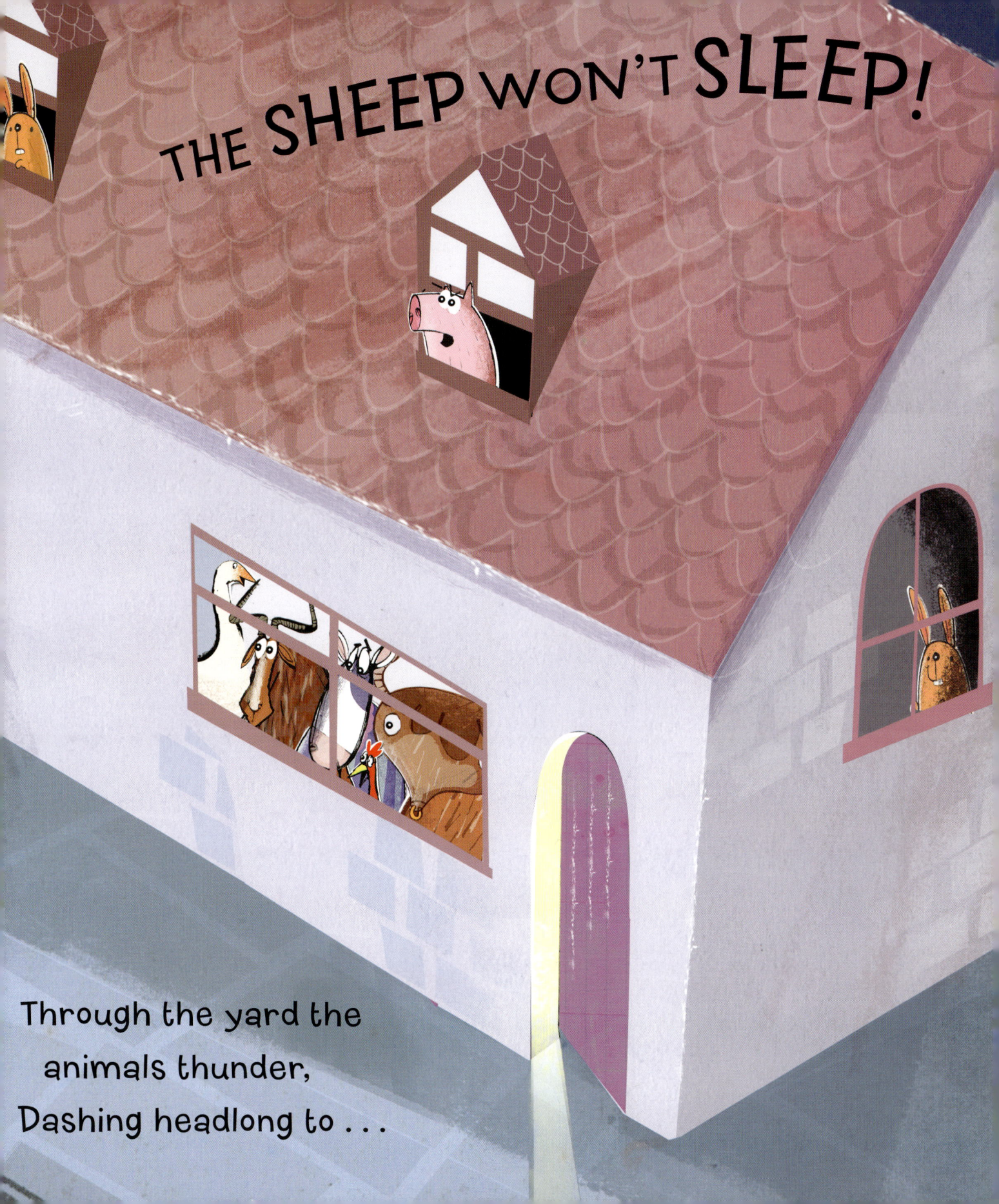

Through the yard the animals thunder,
Dashing headlong to . . .

# NINETY NINE?

Where, oh where, can the last sheep be?

Won't you have a search and see?

Asleep in the kennel, safe and sound,
Our last little sheep has been found!

A hundred Sheep AT LAST put to bed,
And a tired old Sheepdog . . .

Zed . . .

Zed . . .

Zed . . .